FREEUSE OFFICE PARTY

A HOTWIFE SHARED

LACEY CROSS

Paperback ISBN: 978-1-960162-31-1

Book Cover by Steph Brothers

CONTENTS

CHAPTER 1

The car pulls up to the curb in front of the office, and my husband Jon kisses me goodbye. "Have lots of orgasms today, Kitten."

I give him my best cheeky grin. "One can hope."

But honestly, how can I not? It's the last day of freeuse at work before Cindy, the receptionist, comes back from vacation and we have to behave—or at least keep the sexy shenanigans behind closed doors. This week has been fabulous, but fairly intense. It might be good that she's coming back. I don't think much actual work was done this week.

I step out of the car, and smooth down my flared skirt before collecting my purse and lunch. Jon waves to me and I blow him a kiss before he takes off. He doesn't usually take me to work, but Mr. Jacobs offered me a party with all the lawyers today, and Jon is going to come back to watch. We're preplanning for once so we don't have two cars here, and he'll drive me home after the party...assuming the lawyers agree to Jon being there.

The office is eerily still like it's been every morning this week, the usual hum of activity replaced by an almost palpable tension. No one is around the reception area, but the hair on my arms raises as if someone is watching me. I expect one of the lawyers to pop out of their office and fuck me at any second.

I barely have time to set my purse down before my phone's intercom buzzes.

Mr. Jacobs' voice cuts through the silence. "Miranda, my office in five minutes."

I get an immediate jolt of adrenaline. "Yes, sir."

I straighten my blouse again, double-checking that the top two buttons are undone to show a hint of cleavage. Actually—I unbutton another one so that the lace of my pink bra is peeking out. Jon chose this outfit for me, and I know he'd approve.

Since I have five minutes to kill, I turn my computer on and put my lunch in the break room fridge. When I get to Mr. Jacobs' office, the door is open and he's sitting at his desk.

"Close the door." He's using his stern tone that makes me instantly wet.

I do as I'm told, and stand in front of his desk with my hands clasped, waiting for his next move.

"Are you ready for your last day as our freeuse office slut?" He leans back in his chair. His gaze travels over me, and I fight the urge to fidget. "If you please us today—if you're a good girl—we'll all fuck you after work in the conference room."

Hmm, does he REALLY want me to behave? I fight the urge to smile, and tilt my head to the side. "And if I'm not a good girl?"

Mr. Jacobs' lips twitch with amusement. "Then we send you home without an orgasm. Simple as that."

Wait, does this mean I won't come at all today until the party? This was not part of my mental plan. I bite my lip, considering. He's manipulating me, and we both know it. But I'm eager to play along. I want this—I want them. But we need to talk about Jon. Shit, he better be okay with Jon watching.

I undo another button on my blouse and trail my fingers along my collarbone, making sure Mr. Jacobs is watching. "All of that is agreeable, but Jon has a demand."

Mr. Jacobs raises an eyebrow and I know he's waiting for me to elaborate.

"Jon wants to watch." Nerves flutter in my stomach. This is a deal breaker. No Jon, no party. "He wants to be here when you all use me."

Mr. Jacobs' keeps his face neutral. "Watch, hmm?" he muses. "And what makes you think we'll agree to that?"

I shrug. "Because you want to fuck me more than you want to deny Jon the pleasure of watching. And let's be honest, you'll get off on him watching too."

At least I hope so. I don't actually know if Mr. Jacobs has an exhibitionism kink, but we did a conference room fuck-fest years ago with Jon watching over video, and everyone seemed to enjoy that–including Mr. Jacobs.

His lips twitch again, and I know I've hit the mark. He's amused by this—the negotiation, the power play. It's all part of the game.

"You're right, but I'm not going to make it easy for you. If Jon wants to watch, that's fine. But you have to earn it. Understood?"

My heart pounds from excitement. I'm not exactly sure what they'll ask of me, but I always revel in whatever kinky thing my bosses come up with. "Understood, sir."

He stands up and moves behind me. "Then let's start with a reminder of who's in charge."

His hands slide down my sides, fingers brushing lightly against my blouse. Even through the thin fabric, his touch sends tingles of electricity through me.

He turns me to face him. "Take off your blouse."

I comply, and unbutton it, letting it fall to the floor. His eyes dip to the pink lace of my bra, and my nipples instantly harden.

"Beautiful," he says, his gaze lingering appreciatively. With one fingertip, he traces the delicate lace, the featherlight contact raising goosebumps across my skin. A mischievous smile plays at the corner of his mouth.

"I think I'll keep this," he says, scooping up my blouse from where it fell. "You can spend the day just like this. Give everyone at the office something to truly appreciate."

"Yes, sir." I really hope no clients stop by the office today.

"Good. Now get to work. You have a lot to do before 5 p.m." I nod, turning to leave, but he stops me. "And Miranda? Don't disappoint us."

I glance back at him. "Wouldn't dream of it, sir."

There's an extra sway in my hips as I leave his office. Dang it, why didn't he spank me already? I probably should have been bratty to start the day off properly.

As soon as I'm at my desk, I pull out my phone and text Jon.

Miranda:

> Babe, the party is at 5. I have to be a good slut today, or no party.

His response is almost immediate.

Jon:

> Then I guess you better be the best office slut ever. I want to see you take on all the lawyers.

I don't even try to stop my laugh. This is going to be fun, but there's one thing I need to know. My fingers hover over the keypad, hesitating for a moment before I type out the question.

Miranda:

> What if one of them wants to fuck my ass?

I hit send and wait, drumming my fingers nervously on the desk. My pulse quickens as I think about having all my holes filled today. Anal's not an all-access pass kind of thing. After I crossed one of Jon's boundaries a few years ago, Jon and I have a deal. My ass is his territory, and he decides who gets the key.

My phone buzzes, and I glance down.

Jon:

> I'm willing to share my hole today because it's a special day.

A flush warms me. Jon's willingness to share this part of me today makes me feel even more cherished, in a messed-up way. My fingers fly over the keys.

Miranda:

> I promise to make you proud. Love you so much.

My heart flutters with anticipation and affection. Today is going to be incredible.

CHAPTER 2

The clock on my computer says 8:30 a.m, and the day stretches out before me. I'm uncertain what to expect. Am I going to do real work today? I'd rather not, but I'm alone in my little corner and the office is quiet. If I'm going to work without my blouse on, the least they could do was be around to admire me.

My instant messenger on my computer pings.

Mr. King:

Come to my office.

Oooh, thank god. I stand and adjust my skirt, acutely aware of how exposed I am without my blouse. What my bosses haven't found out yet is that I'm wearing matching pink panties, along with a black garter belt and stockings. A seam runs down the back of each leg, adding a touch of elegance. Jon wanted me to be a proper freeuse office toy today, and that included wearing fancy undergarments.

My black high heels sink into the carpet as I make my way to Mr. King's office. I should probably ditch the shoes at some point, but I want a couple of the lawyers to see me wearing them first.

Mr. King's door is slightly ajar, and he's seated at his desk. He doesn't speak until I close the door behind me.

"Lock it."

I want to give him a cheeky, 'yes, sir,' but I keep it in. He's the lawyer I've fucked the most at work recently, and I know his MO now. He has a sadistic streak and he likes to provoke my bratty side.

I lock the door and when I turn back to him, he's standing. I take a moment to admire his broad shoulders—there's just something about a guy in a tailored suit that revs my engine and now that I know what Mr. King can do to me? Oh yeah, me and my slutty pussy are willing to jump through a lot of hoops to get what he offers.

His gaze lingers on my breasts before scanning the rest of me. I can feel the slick, wet heat between my legs, and I ache to be touched.

"You look..." He pauses, his eyes narrowing as he takes me in. "Fuckable."

I fight the urge to rub my thighs together in anticipation. "Thank you, sir."

Having a fabulous orgasm would start the day off nicely.

He smirks, and a longing pulls at my core. "Take off your skirt."

I deftly unzip my skirt, and let it pool at my feet. He's the first one who gets to see the garter belt.

"Turn around," he commands.

I pivot slowly, giving him the full view. When I'm facing him once more, I find his expression unreadable, a practiced blank slate from years of negotiations.

He moves behind me like a predator. His fingers graze my hip before cupping my ass. I moan softly at the contact, and my panties grow damp. Heck, at this rate, I'll have my orgasm before 9 a.m. and still have 3 more lawyers to go.

"You want to come, don't you?"

"Yes, sir."

He chuckles. "Too bad. You're not going to."

Dammit. I frown. "But—"

"No buts," he cuts me off, and the sharpness only makes me want him more. "You're here to please us, remember? And right now, it pleases me to deny you."

Fuuuck. He knows exactly what he's doing. It's infuriating and exhilarating. And by how wet my panties are now, I'm clearly getting off on this.

He gestures to a stack of folders on his desk. "File these for me."

I'm caught off guard by the sudden shift. "File them in the cabinet here?"

"Yes. You're going to work while I use you."

My thoughts whirl as I start sorting them alphabetically. I keep imagining him fucking me as soon as I reach for the bottom drawer, so I'm distracted enough that I keep fumbling the order.

He huffs impatiently and applies firm pressure to my shoulder, making me bend over his desk until my face is squished against the pile of folders. Yeah, okay, this wasn't exactly what I expected, but it'll do.

"You like knowing I can use you whenever and however I want, don't you?" I hear the clink of his belt buckle and the sound of him pulling down the zipper of his slacks.

"Yes, sir," I whisper, while a ping of excitement rushes straight to my pussy.

He nudges my panties to the side, the lace stretching as he exposes me. He positions the tip of his cock against my pussy, and I sigh and close my eyes as he thrusts into me slowly.

His thick cock stretches me wide, every ridge and vein massaging my slick pussy walls. I take him deeper and his hips press firmly against my ass. He doesn't rush—he fucks me slowly, each thrust measured, and I shake with the effort to hold back.

"You feel so fucking good." His voice is strained. "So tight around me."

He picks up the pace. Delight spirals from my pussy, but I know I can't come. Not yet. Not until he says so. It would just be momentary bliss, and then he'd find a new devious way to torture me.

He slams against me, and I yelp in shock and pleasure. The longer he fucks me, the more I stop caring about future punishment.

"Please, sir, I need—"

He cuts me off. "Oh, you need to come? That's unfortunate."

Damn him. My groan of frustration ends in a squeak as he smacks my ass. My eyes fly open. The sting creates a rush of ecstasy and I almost come all over his cock.

"Ooooh, god!" I cry out as he spanks me again, harder this time.

I grasp the side of the desk tighter and fight to hold back my orgasm. I don't want to risk punishment by coming.

"I'm going to use this tight pussy until I've had my fill. And then you're going to thank me. Do you understand?"

"Yes," I mewl out as he hammers into me. My cheek is still plastered against a manila file, and my vision swims from pleasure as I stare at the file cabinet across the room. If the plan was to make me a fucktoy first thing, Mr. King is doing a superb job of it. This is what I crave occasionally that my husband has a difficult time satisfying. I always know that Jon loves me. But Mr. King? Yeah, I'm being used. It's amazing.

"You're going to work like this all day," he growls as he pumps in and out of me. "Aching, desperate, and denied. And if you're a good girl, maybe—just maybe—you'll get to come at the end of the day."

I press my lips together, trying to hold back a whimper. He seizes my forearms, pulling them back and forcing me to rise up from the desk just enough that my nipples rub against the wood through my bra. The additional pleasure is almost my undoing as he fucks me harder.

His cock throbs inside me. He's close—I can tell by the way his breath hitches and his grip on my forearms tightens.

"Fuck, so good." He groans, a guttural sound, right before his cock pulses. He explodes, his hot cum filling me, coating my insides, and making me squirm.

He lets go of my arms to clasp my waist, holding me still while he unloads. I'm almost surprised when I don't come just from the warmth of his seed inside me. My pussy milks every last drop, as if draining his balls is my job.

"Good girl." His breath is ragged as he removes his cock. He slaps my ass and I don't even squeak. I'm too fuzzy-headed. "Now get back to work."

Oh god. I straighten up and look around the room. What am I even doing? I notice my skirt on the floor—oh yeah, I need that. I put it on and fasten it the best I can. I'll fix it later.

"Don't forget the folders," he grouses as he sits down at his desk.

My hands shake as I try to focus on gathering them into a pile. It's impossible. All I can think about is my throbbing clit and his cum dripping out of me.

"Mr. King," I say softly. "Please—"

He cuts me off. "Have you had breakfast?"

I blink in confusion, trying to recall the morning's events. Then I remember that Jon made me oatmeal and fruit before work, insisting I needed the energy for the day ahead.

"Yes," I reply, the memory of Jon's caring gesture warming me.

Mr. King nods and stands up. "Come with me," he says gently, holding on to my arm and leading me to the break room.

The change in his demeanor throws me off, but I follow without question. He grabs a bottle of water from the fridge and hands it to me. "You will drink all of this."

He escorts me back to my desk, his hand on the small of my back. He sits me down, his touch lingering for a moment before he pulls away.

"Drink up," he says, and then he turns and leaves.

I take a sip of the water, the cool liquid soothing my dry throat and perking me up a bit. It really did take me a bit to warm up to Mr. King when he joined the firm, but damn does that man know how to make me a submissive little slut. He ended up being the perfect addition to the firm.

The wetness between my legs and the way my damp panties cling to me are maddening. I'm going to be wrecked by the end of the day. And I can't wait.

CHAPTER 3

The morning crawls by, an endless tug-of-war between arousal and frustration. I cleaned up in the bathroom, but I swear that Mr. King's cum is still leaking out of me every time I shift in my chair. Yeah, it's probably just wishful thinking. After a trip to the copy machine, I kick off my heels—two of the lawyers saw me in them, and that's enough. My panties stick to my skin, the lace rubbing against my swollen pussy with each movement. I'm a needy slut, and it's barely past 11 a.m.

My instant messenger pings, providing a blessed distraction.

Mr. Daniels:

> Come to the break room right now.

I try not to skip down the hall in excitement. Mr. Daniels is already there, leaning against the counter, arms crossed over his broad chest. He's not wearing a suit jacket, and I'm reminded again of how attractive he is. His rich, warm brown skin seems to glow under the break room lights, and he flashes me that amazing smile of his. His eyes, oh those eyes—crinkly at the corners and so full of lust—meet mine, and desire flutters in my stomach. After attending the conference with him yesterday, I'm looking at him in a new light. He's definitely grown more confident since he first joined the firm, which only makes him sexier.

"This is a delightful view," he says, his deep voice filling the room. His gaze travels over me, taking in my bra, my stockings, the way my nipples strain against the lace. "Come here."

I move closer, and he strokes my cheek with his fingers before trailing his hand down to my collarbone. His featherlight touch sends a shiver down my spine.

"I've been waiting for my turn with you all morning." His thumb tickles the skin on my breast just above my bra. "I hear you're being a good slut so far. So obedient."

"Thank you, sir." There's a fresh surge of wetness between my legs and I'm ready to worship his cock.

He chuckles, and turns me around, folding me over the break room table until I'm resting on my elbows. Oh, hello. He pulls my skirt up and presses up against my ass.

"I bet knowing that we can fuck you whenever we want today makes you wet."

"Yes," I whisper, and spread my legs in the hopes it entices him to take me right here.

His fingers slip beneath the lace of my panties, and he rubs my swollen clit. Jesus, if he doesn't fuck me soon, I'm going to go insane. He circles my clit slowly, his touch light and teasing. I clutch the side of the table and rock backwards.

When he inserts two fingers inside me and starts finger fucking me, I quiver as I try to hold back my orgasm. I'm peeping out in distress and the delight threatens to overwhelm me. "Oh, no, no. I'm going to come!"

He stills his hand and laughs. "No, you won't."

He removes his hand from my pussy and I almost groan. Fuck, this is worse.

"Come with me." He makes sure I can walk on my own, and I follow him to his office.

He shuts the door and sits at his desk. "Come over here and get on your knees. It's time for you to be a cockwarmer while I make a phone call."

Uh, fuck, that's hot. I sink to the floor in front of him, thankful I'm not wearing my heels any longer. He unzips his pants, freeing his cock, and I stare at his massive size. How did I get so lucky to work with four lawyers who all have impressive packages? Well, the real luck is that I have a husband willing to let me play with these gorgeous cocks. It's like winning the slut lottery.

"Open," he says firmly.

I part my lips, and he fits his cock into my mouth. I moan around him, the taste of his precum salty on my tongue. He presses on the back of my head, guiding my movements as I take him deeper. I relax, letting him fuck my mouth.

"That's it." He groans. "I always love using your mouth."

Always? Does he think about it outside of work? God, I hope he does. I moan in pleasure, the vibration making him twitch in my mouth. He twists my hair tighter, and suddenly, he holds my head still. His cock is still in my mouth but he's not thrusting.

He picks up his desk phone, dialing a number as I kneel there. I hear the ringing, and then a faint voice on the other end greeting him.

"Yes, this is Mr. Daniels," he says, sounding professional and calm, as if he isn't sitting there with his cock in my mouth. "I need to reschedule our meeting to next week."

My mind spins. I concentrate on not drooling on the cock occupying my mouth. This is humiliating, yet oddly exhilarating.

"No, Wednesday won't work." He shifts slightly, and I take the opportunity to change my position, trying to find a more comfortable angle. "I have a meeting scheduled with a client that day."

I curl my tongue around his shaft, and he grips my hair tight enough to make my scalp tingle. "Hold on a sec."

He presses mute on the receiver and looks at me. "Behave. You're just warming my cock. Don't even use your tongue."

Shit. I mumble, "Yes, sir," around his cock and then he unmutes the phone.

"I checked my calendar. Thursday works," he continues. "So, how have you been?" He now has a casual, friendly demeanor. "It's been a while since we caught up."

Oh god, what the fuck? I try to swallow, but some of my saliva runs down his cock. This is filthy, and I love it. I want to suck on him and clean him up, and just kneeling here while he chats as if he has no care in the world is the perfect blend of hot and annoying.

"That's great to hear," he says, laughing softly at something the other person says. "Yeah, we should definitely have lunch sometime soon." He ends the call and smirks down at me. "Okay, where were we?"

I hold still, waiting for him to give me instructions that I can move. He pushes my head down and I take that as a sign to start sucking again. I hollow my cheeks and get to work, but he takes over almost immediately and holds my head in one place as he flexes his hips to fuck my mouth. He groans at the moment his hot, salty release strikes the back of my throat. I struggle to swallow it all.

When he pulls me off his cock, I'm panting. He tucks himself back into his slacks. A mixture of cum and saliva spills down my chin. Quickly, I wipe it away with my fingers, then suck them clean, savoring every last bit.

He sighs, and I can tell he's pleased. My thoughts are jumbled. Jon is going to love hearing this part of the story.

He stirs and cups my face gently. "I think you've earned a reward."

I almost coo. Mmm, I like rewards. He lifts me to my feet and then boosts me up onto his desk. Oooh, is he going to fuck me? Can he even get it up again this quickly?

He forces me to lie back, but instead of fucking me, he sits down on his chair and drapes my legs over his shoulders. I gasp as he pulls my panties to the side.

His breath is hot against my pussy. "You're so fucking wet. I can see how much you need this."

"God, yes," I whimper.

He doesn't tease me and just dives in. I moan as he licks the length of my pussy and laps my clit. He devours me like I'm a five-star meal. My orgasm builds quickly, and I don't think I'll be able to stop it.

"Come for me." His voice is muffled against my pussy, but I'm still able to hear him. "Come all over my face."

As soon as he gives me permission, my orgasm hits. I'm drowning in a sea of bliss as he licks and sucks me through it. He's relentless and I'm almost too sensitive by the time he stops.

He stands up and wipes his mouth with the back of his hand. "You did so well, Miranda."

"Thank you, sir." I smile weakly, my body still buzzing with the aftermath of my orgasm.

He helps me sit up, and once he sees I'm steady, he says, "Now, clean yourself up. You've got more work to do today."

I hop off the desk and give him a little grin. "Yes sir, right away sir."

I sashay my way to the restroom. Thank god one of them let me come. I can think clearly after the orgasm, and my pussy tingles at the thought of what the next lawyer might do to me.

There's only five more hours until the party.

CHAPTER 4

I plop down into my office chair, my body humming like I've stuck my finger in an electrical socket. My bra feels too small, thanks to my tender breasts. Only one orgasm so far, and it's already past lunch. My bosses are playing hot potato with my libido, and I'm fairly certain all of them—except Mr. Daniels—are conspiring to keep me needy all damn day.

I peek at my phone, debating whether to shoot Jon a text. He's probably up to his elbows in work, but I know he'll want a status update. I unlock the screen and start tapping away.

Miranda:

Babe, I've only come once. I'm dying over here.

I can almost hear his teasing tone when he replies.

Jon:

Aww, poor kitten. Being a good office slut?

Miranda:

The best. Oh, and they seem to be taking turns. Mr. Parks still hasn't fucked me.

Jon:

Maybe he's got something special planned.

Hopefully it's his cock or fingers in my ass. As soon as Jon said he'd share my ass, I turned into my sluttiest self—well, let's be honest, I was mostly already there. But now all I can think about is having Mr. Parks' cock in my ass so I can drip cum from every hole.

Miranda:

I don't need anything special, I just need more orgasms.

I pout, wishing he was here to appreciate my pain.

Jon:

I love it when you get all cranky.

Miranda:

You're the best. Now stop distracting me. I'm trying to work!

Jon:

You do that, and don't spend too much time imagining me sitting here stroking while thinking about watching you get fucked by your bosses.

A thrill zips through me. He always knows how to rev my engine, even from afar. I doubt he's actually stroking at work...right?

I text him some heart emojis and stash my phone in my purse. Dang, I wish Jon were here right now and watching all of this, but we'll have fun for days while I tell him everything that happened. First, I have to survive the rest of the day.

Right on cue, my instant messenger dings. It's Mr. Parks.

Mr. Parks:

Come to my office.

Hell yeah. A delicious ache between my legs roars to life as I head for his office. His door is closed, and I knock.

"Come in."

Mr. Parks is at his desk, and his glasses perched on his nose give him a sexy, geeky look. My pussy clenches like she thinks she's going to get spanked, and I almost giggle from excitement. Okay, so yeah, I've been really looking forward to spending time with Mr. Parks again. He's the only lawyer who hasn't fucked my pussy yet this week.

"Lock the door. We don't want anyone walking in on this."

Uh, yeah…probably not. But is one of the other lawyers going to really walk in? I do as I'm told, and then stand there at the door, fidgeting. I'm so desperate right now, I could just lie down on his desk and beg him to do me. I'm not sure I have coyness in me right now.

"Come here," he finally says.

I step closer, my legs wobbling slightly. He leans back in his chair, eyes roving over me and I'm tempted to turn around so he can admire me from behind.

"Are you ready for me to fuck your ass today?" His tone is almost conversational, which makes this all dirtier.

Happy butterflies swirl in my stomach, and I keep my answer simple. "Yes."

"Good." He smiles, and I expect him to tell me to bend over.

He doesn't.

"But first there's a quiz."

Uh, what? "Quiz?"

"If you answer correctly, you can come when I fuck your ass. Answer wrong..." He leaves the rest unsaid.

My brain's scrambled from the day's festivities. But heck, maybe they'll be easy questions. "Okay. Ready when you are."

He motions me over to him. "One more thing. You'll be giving me a blowjob during the quiz. Now get on your knees."

Well, there goes my chance of an orgasm. No way am I going to be able to think with his cock in my mouth. I kneel between his legs and he pulls his cock out.

I'm a thirsty slut and he doesn't even have to tell me to open my mouth. I drop down onto his shaft, relishing the musky taste of his hard length. I really am in office slut mode, and if one of them told me to crawl naked to the break room to suck his cock, I'd do it.

I close my eyes and spend a moment familiarizing myself with his cock again, and savoring how it throbs in my mouth. He sucks in a breath when I flick the tip of my tongue along the veins, and then tugs on my hair to make me release him.

"What's the capital of France?"

Oh, this is easy. "Paris."

"Correct." He fucks my mouth again for a few minutes before pulling out. "Chemical symbol for gold?"

I try to think. "Um... Au?"

He thrusts back into my mouth, holding me there as he uses me. When he pulls out, I'm wooly-headed and gasping for air.

"Final question. What's 2,417 times 24?"

I hesitate, my thoughts sluggish like I'm wading through mud. Math? Seriously? The numbers jumble in my head. "I... I don't know."

"Two out of three isn't good enough. You don't get to come." He stands up, his chair rolling back with a soft squeak. "Bend over the desk."

I stumble to my feet and do as he requests, turning my head and resting my cheek against the smooth wooden surface. Knowing in advance I won't come pings the part of me that loves being a fucktoy. Using my ass for his pleasure only is the right kind of wrong.

He runs a hand over the fabric of my panties and pulls them down just far enough to expose my ass. He doesn't bother unhooking my garters.

"Such a pity you won't come. I wanted to make you scream while I fucked your ass. But rules are rules."

I imagine how much ecstasy it would take to make me scream and my nipples harden. I mean, I might come...Fuck it, I'm going to come if I can.

I hear the click of a cap opening, and then feel the cool lube. He takes his time, circling my entrance with a slick finger, making sure I'm prepared. This reminds me of years ago, that first day he brought me into his office and found out I'd never had anal sex. He just teased me with his finger, and made me eager to try it.

One of his fingers stretches me out. I moan as he adds more lube and a second finger. He pumps in and out while I adjust to having something in my ass. His cock is against my thigh, and he smears pre-cum along my skin.

"Maybe I should make you beg for it in the ass."

It sounds like he's talking to himself, so I stay quiet while pushing back against his fingers. The pressure is always a little uncomfortable at first, but it quickly turns to delight. God, I want another orgasm. He needs to just stick his cock in right now.

When he moves his free hand down to rub my clit, I quiver from pleasure and finally crack. "Please, Mr. Parks, I need your cock in my ass." I'm not above begging when I want something.

He chuckles. "That's more like it. I love it when you're a slut for an ass fucking." He removes his fingers, and a moment later the blunt head of his cock is pressing against my back entrance. He enters slowly, stretching me open around his thick shaft. The burn of the initial penetration gives way to pleasure as he eases inside.

"That's a sexy sight."

I look back at him, and his eyes are fixated on his cock sinking into my ass. I get naughty pleasure from imagining how dirty that looks from his view.

He grunts once he's fully seated and pauses, letting me acclimate. I flex my ass muscles for funzies, and we both moan as he pulls all the way out. He thrusts back in quickly and I squeal from the delight. Shit, fuck, he needs to keep doing that.

"So tight, so perfect," he grunts as he fucks me steadily.

I can only focus on the increasing ecstasy, and I don't know how long he drills into me. Everything is amazing. I jiggle my ass, trying to get as much pleasure as I can. I have to come before he does.

He picks up speed. "That's it, take my cock like the good little anal slut you are."

His words are punctuated by the slap of skin against skin as he pounds into me. His cock drags along my inner walls, and I'm so close to coming. My clit throbs, begging for attention,

"Yes, I'm an anal slut. Use my ass however you want." I'm babbling, too turned on to care about how desperate I sound.

He withdraws again until just the tip remains inside me before slamming back in. The force of his thrusts rocks the desk, and I have to brace myself against the surface to keep from being shoved forward.

"Please, Mr. Parks, I need to come. I'm so close." I'm practically sobbing now, and trembling with the effort of holding back my orgasm.

"No coming." He reaches around to rub my clit, and I nearly scream in rapture. He circles the nub mercilessly as he continues to fuck my ass.

"Please, I can't hold back. I'm going to come." My pussy spasms around nothing, and I'm going to explode any second.

"Too late," he groans as his cock throbs. Oh god, noooo. His warm seed coats my insides, and I'm twitching from the stolen orgasm.

He pulls out and sits in his chair. "Fuck, that was good."

I can only whimper in response as his cum drips out of my well-fucked hole. At least I got that, even if I didn't come.

He pulls a container of wet wipes from his desk and I sigh in relief when he cleans me up. After he uses one on himself, he puts his cock back into his slacks and then helps me to my feet. I stagger a bit, and I hold onto his waist while he pulls my panties up.

"Now thank me for fucking your ass and not letting you come."

His words immediately make me more submissive and I give him what he wants. "Thank you, Mr. Parks, for fucking my ass. And thank you for not letting me orgasm."

His eyes crinkle with satisfaction. "Anytime, Miranda. Now get back to work before one of the other partners comes looking for you."

I nod, and as I head to the door, he calls out. "And drink more water and eat a snack. Keep your strength up for later."

"I will."

His cum leaks out of my ass the entire walk back to my desk. There's only one cock I haven't had inside me yet today. Is Mr. Jacobs going to fuck me before the party?

Chapter 5

At about 3 p.m. Mr. Jacobs intercoms me and tells me to come to his office. I haven't done much work all day. Between the lawyers using me, I sat at my desk and blanked out while imagining being spit roasted by them.

When I get to his office, one glance from Mr. Jacobs has my heart racing.

"Shut the door," he orders.

My breath catches as I close it. If he didn't plan on using me, he'd leave it open, right? Cause really, closing the door is just for show—it's another way for him to control me.

He's sitting behind his desk, and his eyes devour me. I squirm under his stare and heat blossoms in my stomach.

"I heard you were quite the little slut today."

I'm not sure how to answer. I was a slut, and it was wonderful. But I'm not sure if that's going to get me what I want, so I try to deny it. "N-no, sir. I was a good girl."

Heh, a good girl at being a slut.

"Strip."

Mmm, oh yeah, I'm getting fucked, but just as added insurance, I take my time removing my skirt, since he still has my blouse. I lift my foot onto the chair, and toy with the clasps of my garter belt before I unhook one of my stockings. Mr. Jacobs stares at my legs. I know what he wants—and I'm more than willing to give it to him.

Slowly, I roll down the silk stocking, and the smooth fabric glides over my skin inch by inch as I reveal more of my bare leg. His gaze tracks the movement, and I get a zing of pleasure knowing I have his full attention. I finally slip the stocking off my foot, letting it dangle from my fingers for a moment before dropping it to the floor.

I switch legs, repeating the process with the other stocking. The room is silent except for the soft rustle of fabric and my own heartbeat pounding in my ears. I can sense the heat of his stare, the anticipation in the air.

Next, I remove the garter belt and it joins the stockings on the floor. Reaching behind my back, I unhook my bra and let the straps slip down my arms. I hold the cups in place for a moment, prolonging the reveal, before letting the bra fall away completely.

My breasts are full, yet perky, and I pull at the nipples while he watches with lust. Oh yeah, he wants me as much as I want him. I saved my panties for last because I know how to get him riled up. I turn around, facing away from him and hook my thumbs into the waistband. I slowly pull my panties down, leaning forward to give him a clear view of my ass as the fabric glides down my legs. Stepping out of them, I kick them aside with a playful flick of my foot. For the finale, I shimmy my hips before straightening up and facing him.

The desire in his eyes matches my raw need. He stands up and moves behind me. "Bend over. It's time for your spanking."

Fuck yeah. I position myself at his desk, resting on my forearms so I can look over my shoulder at him. I wiggle my ass to tempt him. My breasts are heavy, my nipples tight, and everytime they skim across the cool surface of the desk, it sends sparks of pleasure straight to my throbbing clit.

"Spread your legs," he orders, and I widen my stance.

His hand strikes my flesh, sharp and sudden. I gasp, the sting spreading like wildfire. He waits a beat, then strikes again. Each smack is a jolt of pain that melts into pleasure while my nerves sing.

As he continues to spank me, the tension increases in my core while my breath comes in short gasps. Each impact of his hand resonates through me.

"You're such a good little slut."

The praise makes me tingle and amplifies the delight. He changes his rhythm, alternating between sharp smacks and gentle caresses. The contrast drives me insane until I'm dizzy with need.

Each smack brings me closer to the abyss. A final, firm spank sends me spiraling. I cry with my climax, and pleasure radiates to my fingertips and toes.

His hand stills, resting gently on my heated flesh. "Good girl."

I am a good girl. I'm in a contented haze from the afterglow, and I barely register the rustling fabric as he takes his cock out. He positions himself behind me, and enters me with a single, powerful thrust. I moan as I almost come again. He was my first introduction to being a hotwife many years ago, and the fact that I'm allowed to fuck him again years later is surreal. I've changed since that first time—we all have—but somehow he still knows what I need.

He drives into me and each thrust creates waves of rapture. He reaches underneath me with both hands to play with my breasts, and he lifts me up slightly so he can roll my nipples with his fingers while fucking me.

"Ohhhh god," I moan as I try to fight against coming.

The tension coils again, but just as I'm about to come, he slows his movements. The change in pace leaves me teetering, the orgasm just out of reach. I moan in frustration as he continues to fuck me slowly.

"You don't get to come again," he growls.

Fuckity, fuck, fuck, fuck. He speeds up, and groans when he finally unloads. Pleasure zips through me, but it stops just shy of sending me over the edge. He fucks his cum back into me, and when he's done, it drips down my inner thigh. Oh yeah, I'm a mess, and going to get even dirtier soon.

I'm an odd mix of happy and frustrated when he says, "Work the rest of the day naked. No point in putting clothes back on."

Uh...other than I need my filthy panties to soak up his cum, but I don't argue. I'm not going to do anything that jeopardizes this party—especially knowing he just came and he might be willing to forgo the festivities if I get cranky.

I give him my best cutesy, "Yes, sir," and saunter out of his office, putting an extra sway in my hips for his benefit.

Is it time for this party yet?

CHAPTER 6

The clock hits 5 p.m. and my stomach flutters with excitement. Mr. Jacobs told me to bring Jon back to the conference room once he arrives.

I'm standing up and leaning against my desk when Jon enters the office and finds me. I'm going to keep my personal shame of sitting on a bunch of paper towels for the last hour to myself. They're in the garbage can, so he won't see them.

Jon's eyes widen a fraction when he sees that I'm naked. "Fuck, kitten. You're a goddamn vision."

His approval boosts my confidence. I'm a sexual goddess. "You like?" I turn slowly, giving him the full view.

"More than like." He steps closer, pulling me into a hug. "I'm obsessed. And I'm going to enjoy watching them fuck you before I take you home and remind you that you're mine."

Mmm, I love it when he gets all growly and possessive. He's going to be really worked up when this is over.

I blush with excitement. "They're waiting for us."

"Then let's go."

I lead him to the conference room, even though he knows exactly where it is. The door's open and as we walk into the room, I notice the lights are dimmed. The large table has been moved aside to create an open space. Mr. Jacobs, Mr. King, Mr. Daniels, and Mr. Parks are perched casually against the table perimeter and all eyes are fixed on me.

"On your knees, Miranda," Mr. Jacobs commands, stepping forward.

Oh damn, they're not wasting any time. Jon moves over to a chair that is conveniently placed against the wall to give him a great view of the entire room.

I kneel down gracefully—I've had years of practice by now. Yeah, I'm on my knees often since I love sucking cocks. I lick my lips and study the bulge in Mr. Jacobs' slacks.

"Here's how this is going to go. You're going to suck on each of us, and then we're going to use you however we want because you're still our freeuse slut. You might orgasm, you might not, but you don't have to ask permission."

Okay, yeah, this sounds good. They use me and I can orgasm. I nod quickly and his eyes twinkle.

"And remember you can always use your safeword if this gets too rough."

I appreciate the reminder, but I already know from past experiences that I'm going to love everything they do to me. "Yes, sir."

Mr. King comes over, and takes his cock out of his pants. I guess Mr. Jacobs isn't going to go first like I assumed.

"Open."

My jaw drops down, and I welcome Mr. King's velvety-smooth cock into my mouth. I can see Jon to the side and he's leaning forward with his elbows resting on his knees, a rapt audience.

Being the center of attention, being used and desired, awakens every nerve in my body. I moan around Mr. King's cock as he fucks my throat. The tang of his precum is pleasant and I lick and suck on him, trying to see if I can make him come.

He pulls out before he does, and I pout. Yeah, my new goal is to make one of them blow their load in my throat when they didn't mean to.

Mr. Daniels is next, and I'm hungry for him. The men are only pulling their cocks out and not fully stripping, which somehow seems filthier. He barely has his out before I throw myself onto it with gusto. He grips my head firmly, forcing me to slow down as he guides me.

Again, the feeling of being used gives me a rush of delight. I know there is affection between us all—even me and Mr. King—but it's different from when Jon uses my mouth. Even though we've talked about boundaries, there's a tiny bit of uncertainty when I allow the lawyers to use me, which makes it even hotter. But having Jon here allows me to relax and really let go.

Mr. Daniels releases his grip to pull his cock out, and I'm left panting, my lips swollen and slick. Jon's gaze is on me. He's enjoying this and knowing that this is turning him on gives me an illicit thrill.

Mr. Parks steps up, his cock already hard and ready. He traces my lips with the head of his cock, teasing me. I dart my tongue out, trying to capture him, but he pulls back. "Eager, aren't you?"

"Please," I moan.

He holds my chin, tilting my head back before feeding me his cock. He's gentler than the others, his movements more controlled, but no less dominating.

My nipples tighten and my pussy spasms. I want more—need more. I ball my hands into fists and hold them against my thighs. Mr. Parks strokes my cheek softly before pulling his cock out without coming.

Mr. Jacobs is last. He puts his hands on my head, and guides me as he thrusts slowly into my throat. I gag slightly, but I'm able to take him. He fucks my mouth steadily, using me for his pleasure.

Jon's gaze is like a physical touch, searing my skin. It spurs me on, makes me want to take more, be more. I'm needy and aching to be fucked.

Mr. Jacobs pulls out, and a string of saliva sticks to his cock. I look up at the four of them, pleading. "Please fuck me."

They smirk and exchange looks. They know they have me right where they want me—aching, needy, theirs to use.

"I think the freeuse toy forgot that she doesn't get to decide how and when we use her."

It's Mr. King who speaks up and it takes all my willpower not to shoot daggers at him with my eyes.

"I'm sorry, sirs. Please, will you fuck me?" My words are soft and submissive, and I hope they're satisfied.

"That's a better attitude," Mr. King says. "On your hands and knees."

My heart thumps as I shift from kneeling to all fours. They circle me, and anticipation swirls in my stomach. I'm trembling by the time Mr. King kneels in front of me and Mr. Parks behind. Mr. Jacobs and Mr. Daniels lean against the conference table, watching.

Mr. King slides his dick back into my mouth while Mr. Park teases the entrance of my pussy with the head of his cock. I'm so desperate, I want to fuck myself on his cock, but I know better.

"Please," I whimper around Mr. King's shaft. I'm not sure which of them I'm talking to, but I don't care what they do as long as I orgasm.

Mr. Parks pushes inside me, and I'm so wet that he bottoms out easily. I moan as my body stretches to accommodate his cock.

Mr. Parks doesn't waste a second and he fucks me hard and fast. My pussy quakes as his balls slap against my clit.

He spanks my ass. "Don't move."

I'm so close, I'm not going to last much longer. I try to focus on sucking on Mr. King's cock, but it's impossible when Mr.

Parks is pounding me so hard that it's shoving Mr. King's cock further down my throat.

"Look at our little office slut," Mr. Daniels says. "She's going to make you come, isn't she, Mr. Parks? It's amazing when her pussy flutters around me when I'm fucking her."

His filthy words make me moan. I love how degrading it is when they talk about me like I'm just a sex toy. I spent too many years wondering what was wrong with me for wanting this, and embracing this sluttiest side of myself is so fucking wonderful.

Mr. Parks' cock twitches. Oh god, yes, please fill me up. Every fiber of my being is focused on the impending ecstasy. My clit throbs and my nipples ache. I'm a live wire, the sparks threatening to ignite with each thrust.

"Come for me, Kitten." Jon's voice cuts through the fog of my lust.

That's all I need. I scream around Mr. King's cock as my orgasm crashes over me. Pleasure wracks my body, and I'm still coming when Mr. Park's hips stutter momentarily before he slams his cock into me one last time. His hot seed flooding me triggers a new wave of delight.

I'm lost in a sea of ecstasy when Mr. King explodes. I lose control and I can't swallow fast enough. Drool and cum leaks out of the sides of my mouth. I'm completely overwhelmed.

I'm still floating on a cloud of bliss when Mr. King pulls his cock out. The cool air of the conference room brushes against my heated flesh. I can't stop smiling. I'm a well-fucked slut, and it's not over yet.

Mr. Parks withdraws from my pussy, and his cum dripping out of me makes me shiver.

Mr. Jacobs speaks. "Clean him up."

Oh shit. I clamber to my knees again. Mr. Parks stands in front of me with his spent cock covered in our combined wetness. I lick from his balls up his shaft, tasting myself on him. He's still sensitive and I smile when his cock twitches.

Once I've given him a thorough tongue bath, Mr. Parks tucks his cock away and moves aside. Mr. Jacobs calls me over and then pushes me down on the table's surface. My nipples graze the wood as I rest on my elbows.

Mr. Jacobs slides his cock into my pussy. "Fuck, she feels so good."

He pounds into my pussy, and his cock drags against my inner walls. I moan loudly from the pleasure.

Mr. Daniels moves to stand next to my head, and he reaches out to stroke my hair. "You're such a good little office slut." He glances at the other partners. "I wonder how many times we can make her come."

That's it. Mr. Daniels is my favorite lawyer at the moment.

Mr. Jacobs grabs my arms and pulls them behind me. He holds them up and pivots, forcing me off the table so I'm facing Mr. Daniels. Mr. Jacobs picks up speed, and his hips slap against me. My pussy quivers, and I cry out and go limp as another orgasm skyrockets me to another plane of existence.

When I come back to earth, Mr. Daniels' cock is at my mouth, and I gurgle happily around his shaft. Mr. Jacobs grinds against me as he pumps my pussy full of his cum. I'm trembling, and I start wondering how much of this I can take. Can there be too much pleasure?

Mr. Jacobs pulls out, and Mr. Daniels withdraws from my mouth without coming. Mr. King takes over. I'm a rag doll as he moves me over to the table again, sitting me on top of it. Mr. King glides his hand up my thigh, his thumb circling my clit in delicate strokes. I melt against his hand and wrap my legs around his waist, hoping to draw him into me. He laughs and removes his hand and unhooks my legs.

"No you don't. I decide how I'm fucking you."

I rest back on the table while he folds my legs towards my chest. My ass is at the edge and he burrows into my wetness.

"Fuck, so good." He starts pounding me, his eyes fixated on where we're joined.

I'm still tender from my last two orgasms and it doesn't take long before I'm wound tight, my breath coming in shallow gasps.

"Oh god, I'm going to come," I cry out right before my orgasm washes over me. I'm lost in ecstasy, my fingers clawing at the table, seeking something, anything, to ground me. I can't hold on, can't fight against the wave of pleasure that consumes me.

Mr. King fucks me frantically, his cock swelling inside me and then exploding. He twitches as he pumps his cum into my well-used pussy.

When Mr. King pulls out, Mr. Jacobs moves between my legs. "One more," he says, sliding into me. "You can give us one more orgasm."

I can only moan in response. He's not wrong, and within minutes of him fucking me, I'm creaming all over his cock. I'm limp when Mr. Daniels picks me up and carries me over to a chair. He stands me up before sitting down himself.

"Ride me and fuck yourself on my cock."

I can do that. I face the room and lower myself onto his cock. Oh fuck. I'm not going to be able to walk straight tomorrow.

I'm so damn satisfied that it's hard to bounce on him, but I find a rhythm. Every nerve ending is pinged by his thick cock, and I'm not going to last long. He grasps my ass and lifts me up. Jon has a clear view of the chair and I play with my nipples while I fuck myself on Mr. Daniels' cock. Each tweak of my nipples sends a corresponding burst of pleasure from my clit, and my continual moans of "Oh god," are getting louder with every thrust.

"Come on, slut. You've got this." Mr. Daniel's voice is tight and he's clearly trying to hold back his own release.

He reaches down to play with my clit, and I shatter. My pussy quakes around him and I scream out. His cock pulses and he comes, adding to the collection of cum inside of me. I slump back against him, my head resting on his chest as I try to catch my breath.

I've lost count of my orgasms. I'm sweaty, sticky, and cum-filled. And I've never felt better in my life.

Jon pipes up from his chair. "One more time, Kitten. And guys, stuff all her holes."

Ooooh, god. Jon is nasty, and I love it.

Mr. King lies on the floor and they maneuver me over him. His cock is out and I sink down onto him. Fuck, my pussy is sore, but it still feels wonderful. Mr. King's cock stretches me again as I ride him slowly, enjoying the pings of pleasure and knowing there's more to come.

Mr. Parks produces a bottle of lube from his pocket and I lean down to give Mr. King a kiss while Mr. Parks preps me for his cock. My tongue twines with Mr. King's while Mr. Park works the lube into my ass. Within moments, he presses his cock against the tight ring and slowly inserts it. I moan into Mr. King's mouth from the intense pleasure. It takes a bit, but once he's inside me, I'm so fucking full, I feel like I could burst.

This is what happiness feels like, and that connection with Jon is unwavering even with me having two cocks in me right now.

"You good, Kitten?" Jon's voice is raw with emotion.

"So good."

When Mr. Daniels kneels next to me with his cock out, I swallow him down. This is the ultimate fantasy. Three lawyers in all my holes. The guys all fuck me and the pleasure makes my head spin. I didn't think I had another orgasm in me, but this is taking me to a place I've never been before. All my nerves sing in delight and it's heavenly.

"I think she needs all our cum at once," Mr. Daniels says, as he pulls out.

I don't know how they plan to do that, but at this point, I don't care what they do to me.

"Do you want to be covered in cum, slut?" Mr. Jacobs asks as he steps up next to me.

"Yes, please." I want it all. I want to be marked by them, to wear their cum on my skin. They have me so turned on that I might orgasm the moment they cover me in cum.

"Then beg for it. Tell us how much you want it." Mr. Jacobs commands.

I look up at him from under my eyelashes. "Please, I need your cum. Cover me in it." Begging the lawyers for their cum drops me into the darkest recess of my soul. A place where I'll do or say anything. "I'm a filthy office slut, and I'm here to be used. Please use me and paint me with your cum." I'm begging, the words pouring from me in a torrent of need.

Mr. Jacobs seems satisfied and says, "Open wide."

I obey, ready to take whatever he gives me. Mr. Jacobs eases into my throat, and as he thrusts into my mouth, the other lawyers focus on me. Their hands roam over my body, teasing and tweaking my nipples, stoking the fire that threatens to consume me.

Mr. Daniels stands next to me, holding his cock over my head while he strokes it. Mr. Jacobs fucks my mouth, and the rhythm of the thrusts in my ass are timed perfectly with Mr. King's cock in my pussy. I'm blissed out from the pleasure. Mr. Daniels' hand moves faster on his shaft and my skin tingles in anticipation of his hot cum on me. I'm so close, my orgasm is just within reach.

Mr. Jacobs' cock twitches as he nears his climax, his grip on my hair tightening. All the guys speed up their movements. Mr. Daniels' hot cum splashes on my face first. His release is the catalyst that triggers the others, and they're quick to follow. Mr. King and Mr. Parks groan and I feel my pussy and ass filled with cum as they explode deep inside me. It triggers my orgasm, and I cry out as my climax rips forcefully through my body. It's a soul-shaking orgasm that leaves me breathless and trembling.

Mr. Jacobs pulls out of my mouth at the last minute and aims for my chest. I shudder when his cum lands on my breasts, dripping down to my belly and thighs.

"Fuck," Mr. Daniels groans, his cock still spurting. His cum drips down my face and sends shockwaves of delight through me. I'm a filthy, cum-covered slut.

When Mr. Parks withdraws from my ass, he helps me climb off Mr. King. They leave me kneeling on the floor and they all step back, admiring their handiwork. I'm a canvas of desire, painted in their pleasure. It's glorious.

"Thank you." My voice is hoarse and I'm not sure if it's from all the cocks I had down my throat, or if it's from my moaning.

They chuckle, their gazes filled with satisfaction. "You're very welcome," Mr. Jacobs says. "We'll see you Monday, but unfortunately with Cindy back we'll have to be discreet if you want more fun."

Mmm, more fun. Jon and I will have to talk about that first. I giggle as the lawyers straighten their clothes. I'm tired and could lie down right here and sleep, but I force myself to stay on my knees.

The lawyers pause over by Jon, but I'm too addled to process what they're saying other than I hear them thank him for sharing me this week. Well, that's nice and respectful after such a filthy event.

Once they're gone, Jon kneels in front of me with a container of wet wipes that one of them must have given him. He cleans me up, and I giggle again as he wipes the cum off my face.

"You're a mess, Kitten," he laughs with me.

"Mmm hmm." I'm floating in my happy place, and indulging in the filthy sensation of their cum drying on me.

When Jon gets up and retrieves my clothes from a chair, I realize one of the lawyers must have put them there without me noticing. Jon dresses me like I'm a doll, all except my garter and stockings. It's sweet.

I'm a sleepy, happy little office slut, and I lean against Jon as we leave. "I love you, Jon."

He kisses the top of my head. "I love you too, Kitten."

Once we're in the car, Jon turns to me. "That was the hottest fucking thing I've ever seen in my life. Thank you."

"Mmm, I'm glad you enjoyed watching." I snuggle into the passenger seat. "I enjoyed the doing."

I close my eyes and drift.

CHAPTER 7

I blink and we're home. If someone had asked me back at the office if I was ready for Jon to fuck me, I would have said no, but the cool air as I step out of the car revives me, and just looking over at Jon's strained expression sends a bolt of desire straight to my core. I'm still humming from the aftermath of the office party, but there's a new energy inside me, one that's reserved only for him.

The moment we step into the house, Jon presses me against the wall and his mouth crashes onto mine. His kiss is demanding, and I melt into it, responding instantly. His tongue twirls with mine, and I can taste his urgency, his need to reclaim me.

"You're mine," he growls. "Mine to love. Mine to protect."

"Yes, yours," I whisper.

"I'm going to fuck you, Kitten. Hard. And you're going to take it because you belong to me."

"Yes, Sir. Please."

Oooh, hell yeah. Beast Jon came out to play. In my most honest moments, this is exactly why I love being a hotwife. I get railed by other men, and then Jon usually goes crazy and gives it to me hard.

He turns me around, pressing my breasts to the wall. His hands caress down my thighs and he hikes my skirt up. He grinds against my ass and I push back, trying to get him inside me.

He slaps my ass sharply, and I yelp from the pleasurable sting. "Who do you belong to?"

"You, Sir," I breathe out. "Only you."

"That's right," he growls while he moves my panties aside. He finds my clit and rubs it until I'm quivering from pleasure. My hands are flat on the wall and I use it as leverage to try and force his fingers inside me.

"Oh god, just fuck me. Please?"

"Oh, Kitten, I plan to," he laughs and pulls his hand out from between my legs. He quickly removes my clothes, dropping them in a pile on the floor. I step out of my heels as he continues. "But let's be clear on one thing..."

He doesn't complete his thought and he picks me up and carries me to the bedroom. He tosses me gently onto the bed and I watch as he strips.

Once he's naked, he crawls over me and nibbles on my neck. "I have two holes to reclaim."

Oh god, I'm about to have my ass stuffed full. "Yes. God, yes."

He sits back on his knees. "Spread your legs."

I eagerly part them and he nestles against me, his cock hard and thick, the tip already glistening with pre-cum. He teases me, rubbing the head of his cock against my clit before lining himself up with my entrance.

He pauses, holding back. He knows how to drive me wild, to make me ache for him, and I'm ready to explode by the time he finally slides inside me.

"Fuck," he groans, his cock stretching me open. He fills me perfectly, and having him inside me is a comfort.

He starts out slow, as if he's reacquainting himself with every inch of my body. I moan as he fucks me, my fingers digging into the sheets. I wrap my legs around him, urging him deeper.

Jon picks up the pace, and I cry out in pleasure from each thrust. He captures my lips in a searing kiss, and my tongue twirls with his. I'm lost in a sea of bliss as he trails kisses along my neck. I'm drowning in him—in us.

He reaches down to find my clit, his fingers working in time with his thrusts. "I want you to come on my cock, Kitten. Now."

It's all I need to fall over the edge. My orgasm crashes over me, my pussy clenching around his cock as waves of delight wash over me. I scream his name, my body quivering with the force of my climax. He continues to pound me through it, his own moans of pleasure mixing with mine. The rapture doesn't end, but just keeps climbing. I'm going to have another orgasm, and soon, and I'm not sure how that's even possible.

He pulls out, and before I can protest, he flips me over and tugs my hips up so I'm on my knees and elbows. His hands are on my ass, spreading me open. He has a bottle of lube. He obviously likes to be prepared. The gel is cold, and I jump as he coats my opening.

"Relax, Kitten," he murmurs as he pushes a finger into my ass. He moves it in and out of me before he adds a second. "You're taking my fingers like a good girl."

"Mmm, so good, Sir."

"I bet," he laughs as he adds a third finger, stretching my asshole to get me ready for him. "I think you're ready."

"Yessss." The word comes out in a long, drawn out hiss.

His lubed fingers leave my ass and the tip of his cock replaces them. "Breathe, Kitten."

I exhale and he pushes inside me. I'm so relaxed from being fucked all afternoon that his cock slides past the barrier easily. He doesn't stop until he's fully sheathed in my ass.

The pleasure is overwhelming. He tugs on my hair gently, and pulls my head up. I have to brace myself on the bed to stay steady. His other hand moves around to my front and he plays with my clit. I'm so sensitive that it hurts, but in the best possible way.

"Such a good girl," he says, his hips moving in small circles, his cock stretching my ass. "I think you can come like this."

I'm not sure I can, and I don't know if I could handle another orgasm. He's not giving me a choice, and I whimper as he thrusts and rubs my clit.

"Come again. Show me who you belong to."

His fingers are relentless on my clit, and I'm on the brink, the pleasure bordering on pain. I want to give him what he wants, but I'm not sure how much more I can take. I'm writhing, my breath ragged as the pressure increases.

"Please." I'm unsure what I'm even asking for, I'm so mentally fucked.

He slows down, but he doesn't stop. "You can do this, Kitten. I believe in you."

His fingers on my clit are short circuiting my brain. My body is on fire and I can't stop it. I don't want to stop it. I want to come apart, to surrender completely to him. I need to give him everything.

The pleasure crests and I scream his name as I come. Waves of ecstasy wash over me, each one more intense than the last. Jon's rhythm falters and he thrusts once, twice more and then stills inside me. He holds me in place as he comes, his cock pulsing in my ass as he fills me. The world fades away, leaving only the two of us.

I collapse onto the bed and he gently pulls his cock out and then lies next to me. He strokes my back gently. "I love you," he whispers. "You're always so good for me."

I'm floating in the haze, and I can't keep the smile off my face.

"You did such a good job today. You made me very happy. I'm so proud of you." He keeps telling me all the ways he loves me and I practically purr with contentment. He's always so sweet and loving after he reclaims me.

I'm drifting to sleep, his words wrapping around me like a warm blanket, his touch a gentle reassurance. He's the only man I love.

"You're mine, Kitten, no matter who I share you with."

"Mmm, yours," I murmur.

He kisses my shoulder. "Sleep a little but then you need to eat."

"Okay, love."

Everything is as it should be, and as my eyelids close, I know that Jon is my forever. Even if he decided to never share me with my bosses again, I'd still love him for all eternity. And I know he loves me the same way.

The End

ABOUT LACEY CROSS

Lacey Cross is a wife sharing erotica writer with over 100 short stories published since she started in 2021. Her stories emphasize the pleasure found from the wife living her best slut life and embracing the hotwife lifestyle. She explores themes of free use, submissive wives with dominant bulls, BDSM...and oh-so-many men.